ANGEL PARK
All-Stars

8

CHAMPIONSHIP GAME

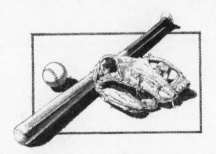

By Dean Hughes

Illustrated by Dennis Lyall

Bullseye Books · Alfred A. Knopf
New York

for Brian Alexander

Library of Congress Cataloging-in-Publication Data
Hughes, Dean, 1943–
Championship game / by Dean Hughes.
p.   cm. — (Angel Park all-stars ; 8)
Summary: Members of the Angel Park community wonder where
Coach Wilkens's loyalties lie when he helps players on rival teams
before the championship baseball game.
ISBN 0-679-80433-1 (pbk.) — ISBN 0-679-90433-6 (lib. bdg.)
[1. Baseball—Fiction.]   I. Title.   II. Series: Hughes, Dean,
1943–   Angel Park all-stars ; 8.
PZ7.H87312Ch   1990
[Fic]—dc20   90-31306
CIP   AC

RL: 2.6
First Bullseye Books Edition: October 1990
Manufactured in the United States of America
10 9 8 7 6 5 4 3 2 1

Look for these books about the
Angel Park All-Stars

★ 1 ★

"Must-Win" Game

"Kenny! Kenny!"

Kenny Sandoval had just gotten out of his dad's car. He turned and saw his friend Jacob Scott running toward him from the baseball diamond.

"You won't believe it! You won't believe it!" Jacob was shouting. He was waving his arms wildly.

"What are you talking about?"

But Jacob didn't answer until he had run all the way up to Kenny, taken a long pause, and flashed his big, split-toothed grin. Then he spoke the words one at a time. "The . . . A's . . . beat . . . the . . . *GIANTS!*"

"*All right!*" Kenny yelled. "I told you, didn't I? I *knew* it could happen."

"You should have seen it. The A's looked like a bunch of all-stars today—almost as good as *us*."

Both boys laughed and then reached high and slapped hands.

"If we win, and the Reds do too, we'll be in a three-way tie for first place," Kenny said.

But Jacob was already looking away from Kenny. He was watching a car that had just pulled into the parking lot. "Come on, it's Harlan. Let's go tell him."

Harlan Sloan was the other rookie on the Angel Park Dodgers' team. The three boys had been friends even before baseball started. But now they were *best* friends.

The season had been great.

Just one thing would make it greater.

The *championship*.

Harlan was just as excited as the other guys when he heard the news. But Kenny's dad brought them back to earth.

"Hey, guys," he yelled to them. "Right now you better concentrate on winning your *own* game. Hustle out there and get warmed up."

"That's right," Jacob said. "Come on. Let's go *sink* the Mariners."

All the Dodgers were psyched when they found out they still had a chance for the season's second-half championship. If they could win it, there would be no play-off, since they were the first-half champs. They would be the champs of the entire season.

But Coach Wilkens made an announcement that not everyone liked. "Kids, I'm going to give the younger players a little more playing time tonight. I'm starting Jacob and Harlan and Lian Jie. And Eddie Boschi will pitch."

"Coach, we shouldn't take any chances," Rodney Bunson said. "We can't afford to lose." Bunson was the Dodgers' star pitcher and hitter.

"I'm not taking chances. Our younger players are playing very well these days."

But Bunson didn't like it. And he liked it even less when he found out he wasn't in the starting lineup.

He had learned not to lose his temper with the coach, but he sat on the bench with his arms folded, looking mad.

The Mariners had made some changes too. The kid who usually played first base—a guy named Rodriguez—was pitching. He was left-handed, and strong, but he was wild.

Henry White led off the game with a walk, and Jacob came up as the second batter.

Kenny knew how excited Jacob was to be batting early in the lineup. He acted like a big-leaguer. He knocked the dirt off his shoes with his bat, and then he rolled his shoulders around to relax.

He swung hard at the first pitch—and missed.

Kenny was kneeling in the on-deck circle. "Come on, Jacob, make him pitch to you!" he yelled. "That ball was high."

Kenny heard Bunson say, "You put Scott in the starting lineup and all of a sudden he thinks he's Babe Ruth."

Jacob was talking to himself, probably doing his own "radio broadcast" of the game, the way he did all the time.

He must have told himself—in his announcer's voice—to be more patient.

He let a couple of pitches go by. Then the pitcher grooved one. Jacob socked the ball into center. And when the fielder bobbled the ball, Jacob kept going and slid into second, safe.

He got up grinning and waving his fists.

Kenny waved back. Now he wanted to bring the runners home.

But the pitcher didn't give him anything to hit. He walked Kenny on four pitches.

The bases were loaded for Sterling Malone. But he got too eager and swung at an outside pitch. He hit a soft grounder to first for an out. At least Henry scored from third.

But then Rodriguez let a pitch get away that hit Eddie Boschi on the shoulder, and the bases were loaded again.

And now Harlan was coming up. Last week he had come through in a big game. He looked confident today.

He let a low pitch go by, and then he held up on one that was outside.

Kenny knew Rodriguez wouldn't want to throw another ball.

Harlan knew it too.

The pitch came in fat and Harlan really *clubbed* it.

It shot into left. The fielder ran hard, but he couldn't cut it off, and the ball bounced all the way to the fence.

Harlan wasn't very fast or he might have had a triple.

But a double was *plenty!*

Three runs scored, and the Dodgers were up by four.

Even Bunson was yelling "Way to go!" to Harlan.

Things only got better. Billy Bacon brought home Harlan with a solid single, and Brian Waters hit a hard grounder that the shortstop booted.

When Lian Jie came up, the Mariners started to laugh. He was the new Taiwanese kid on the team, and he was really small. He didn't look as though he could hit the ball out of the infield.

But the Dodgers knew better, and the Mariners found out.

Lian waited for a pitch in his strike zone and then laced a ball over the second baseman's head.

Another run scored.

At that point the Mariners changed pitchers.

Things settled down after that. But the Mariners never got much going against Boschi, and the Dodgers kept picking up runs.

When Bunson finally got in the game, he could hardly wait to bat. He slammed a monster homer over the left field fence.

Kenny got three hits of his own, and Jacob drove in a run with another single.

So it was a great day for the rookies, and a great day for the Dodgers.

When it was all over, they had won 13 to 5, and they were tied with the Giants for first place.

The whole team stuck around to watch the Reds. But the day wasn't quite perfect.

The hard-hitting Reds didn't play their best, but they played well enough to beat the Padres, 6 to 3.

With one game left in the season, three teams were tied.

And the Dodgers would be playing the Reds on Saturday morning.

The *championship* was in reach.

But another "must-win" game was coming up.

BOX SCORE, GAME 19

Angel Park Dodgers 13   **San Lorenzo Mariners 5**

	ab	r	h	rbi		ab	r	h	rbi
White 3b	4	3	2	0	Cast cf	3	1	1	0
Scott lf	3	1	2	1	Smagler 2b	4	1	1	0
Sandoval ss	4	3	3	1	Amey lf	3	0	1	1
Malone cf	5	1	2	0	Tomas ss	3	0	0	0
Boschi p	3	1	0	1	Antonangeli c	2	1	2	2
Sloan 1b	2	1	1	3	Rodriguez p	3	0	0	0
Bacon c	3	1	1	1	Sullivan 1b	2	0	0	0
Waters rf	4	0	2	1	Cisco rf	1	0	1	1
Jie 2b	1	1	1	1	St. Mary 3b	1	0	0	0
Roper 1b	2	0	1	1	Perez rf	2	2	1	0
Sandia 2b	2	0	1	0	Watson 3b	1	0	1	0
Bunson lf	2	1	2	2	Korman c	1	0	0	0
ttl	**35**	**13**	**18**	**12**		**26**	**5**	**8**	**4**

Dodgers	6	2	2	0	3	0—13
Mariners	0	1	2	1	0	1—5

★ 2 ★

Traitor?

As the Dodgers' players were climbing down from the bleachers, the Reds' big catcher—a guy named Winter—looked up and yelled, "Our next game is *easy!* The Dodgers are *no problem.*"

Sterling Malone yelled back, "Let's see if you talk so big *after* the game!"

Winter had plenty to say about that, but the Dodgers knew better than to answer. Coach Wilkens didn't like that kind of stuff.

But just then Jenny Roper said, "What's the coach doing?"

Kenny spotted Coach Wilkens over by first base, talking to one of the Reds' players.

That was not so surprising. Coach Wilkens was friendly to all the kids.

But he was making a motion, as though he were pitching. Then the kid tried the motion, and Coach Wilkens took hold of his arm and guided it.

"That's the kid who pitched the last couple of innings," Henry White said. "The one who almost lost the game for the Reds."

"I know. But what's Coach Wilkens doing?" Jenny asked.

Everyone knew. But no one wanted to admit it. Kenny could hardly believe what he was seeing.

"He's showing him a better way to throw the ball," Bunson said. "What's he doing that for?"

"I'm not sure," Henry said. "Doesn't he remember we have to play those guys on Saturday?"

"That kid won't pitch," Kenny said. "We'll get Manny Tovar all the way."

"Yeah, but still . . . why does he want to help one of *those* guys?"

Just then the coach said something to Winter, and Winter walked over to him.

The coach went into a crouch, like a

catcher. He showed Winter something about how to hold the glove—and positioning his other hand.

"I don't believe it," Sterling said.

Billy almost choked. He finally coughed out, "How can he help . . . *Winter?*"

Mr. Bunson had just walked up. "What's your coach doing?" he said in a booming voice, like his son's.

"I think he's just . . ." Kenny started, but he wasn't sure exactly what to say. He wanted to believe the coach wasn't doing anything wrong.

"He's helping the team you guys have to play for the championship," Mr. Bunson said. "I don't understand that."

But the younger Bunson had a name for what he was seeing. "He's a *traitor,*" he said.

No one else wanted to go quite that far.

But no one was ready to disagree, either.

Coach Wilkens was leaving by then. But as he walked away, he patted Winter on the shoulder and said something.

"I think he just told Winter 'good luck,' " Sterling said.

"I think I'm going to puke," Billy said—and he started to make retching noises. But no one laughed.

And as they left the park, Kenny could hear Bunson talking to Sterling and Henry. The word "traitor" kept coming up.

The word came up even more at practice the next night.

Before the coach arrived, Bunson spoke to everyone who hadn't stayed for the Reds' game.

"The coach only talked to a couple of their players," Kenny said. "We don't even know what he was saying to them."

Kenny was still trying to think the best of Coach Wilkens.

"He was *showing* them how to play better," Bunson said. "And one of the players was that superjerk Winter."

Danny Sandia almost lost it. "He was coaching *Winter? Winter?!*"

"Come on," Jenny said. "The coach just . . . you know . . ."

"He just *what,* Jenny?" Bunson said. "He just *doesn't care.* That's how he's been all year. He's happy if we win, but he laughs it off if we lose."

"Yeah," Danny said. "That's why he puts little kids in the lineup and leaves the best players on the bench. So what if we lose? He doesn't care!"

"No way!" Jenny said. "The guy has worked his head off to get us where we are."

"Yeah. *Tied* for first," said Bunson. "We should be the champs already."

Kenny didn't buy that at all, and he was trying to think of what to say to Bunson. But just then the coach came driving up. He got out of his van and waved at the players.

"Come and get these bats!" he yelled. "How come you're not stretching?"

Kenny ran over to get the bats. "That's it, Kenny!" Danny yelled after him. "Be his little pet."

Kenny ignored Danny. And he did his best during practice. But the team seemed quiet, and they didn't play so hot. Coach Wilkens chewed them out a couple of times for being lazy.

That didn't go over very well. They were all giving each other looks.

But no one said anything about the coach's helping the Reds' players, and Kenny could tell that he had no idea what the kids were thinking.

Kenny was doing a lot of thinking himself.

At dinner that night he asked his parents for their opinions. It was his mom who was quick to respond. "That doesn't sound right to me," she said.

Kenny's six-year-old brother said, "He's a cheater."

"No, he's not," Kenny said. He was still waiting to hear what his dad would say.

"Well, I think that's the kind of guy he is," Dad said. "He watches a kid play, sees him doing something wrong, and figures he'll help him play better—no matter what team he's on."

"Right before the championship game?"

Mom said. "I can maybe see it in preseason, or during the off-season, or something like that. But what if one of those kids makes the difference in the game tomorrow?"

"Well," Dad said, "some coaches wouldn't do it. Some would. It just depends on how you look at it. Personally, I don't see anything wrong with it."

Kenny tried to accept that. Maybe the coach was just being a good guy.

But then Kenny's mother said, "Well, it may only be Little League, but that championship means everything to these kids. He ought to know that. And he shouldn't stand right there in front of his own team and help any of those bigmouthed *Reds*."

Kenny wished his mom had never said that.

He had been thinking the same thing.

But he didn't want to.

Until now, he had always thought Coach Wilkens was about the greatest guy around.

★ **3** ★

High Tension

Coach Wilkens had his players sit on the outfield grass. In a few minutes the big game with the Reds would be starting.

"Kids, I know how you feel about this game," he said. "It *is* a big one. But let's keep it fun. If we win, great. But if we don't, we still have a chance for the championship."

Kenny had hoped Coach Wilkens would tell the kids to go out there and *kill* the Reds.

"So let's do our best, and let's be good sports, no matter what those Reds' kids start yelling."

"Coach," Bunson said, "could I say something to the players?"

"Sure."

"I mean—with just us players here?"

"Oh. Well . . . yeah. Why not?" Coach Wilkens smiled and walked away.

Bunson got up. "Okay, look," he said. "I don't care what Coach Wilkens says. We're not here just to have *fun*. We're here to kick some *butt*."

"Yeah!" Danny yelled, and everyone jumped up and started yelling with him. Kenny did like the excitement, but he didn't like Bunson's attitude toward the coach.

As the team ran to the dugout, they pounded each other. Brian yelled, "Okay, this is it! Let's get 'em!"

Then Henry White walked out first to face big Manny, the Reds' pitcher—and to face the Reds' big mouths.

Manny was pumped up and throwing *hard*.

But he was high with his first two pitches, and then he bounced one in the dirt. He finally slowed down and got a strike. But just when Henry was ready to tee off on one, the ball sailed high again.

Ball four.

The Dodgers' players yelped with joy as

Henry trotted down to first. "We get Manny today!" Sterling yelled back to the players as he walked to the plate.

The Reds' infield had plenty to say about that. And then they screamed to Manny to *throw strikes.*

"Hey, batta, batta," they chanted as Sterling got ready.

The crowd was already into the game. A lot of the people watching had red shirts on, and they were screaming at Manny to blow the batter away.

But there were just as many in Dodger blue, yelling for Sterling.

Kenny thought it was the biggest crowd of the year. The bleachers were filled, and lots of people had brought chairs to sit along the foul lines.

Manny seemed to be having trouble with so much excitement. His first pitch to Sterling was way high.

Winter, the catcher, ran the ball out to him, and Kenny, who was in the on-deck circle, heard him say, "Come on, Manny. Bring your arm all the way through."

Manny listened. He followed through

better. But the pitch was inside this time. All the Dodgers cheered.

Billy Bacon yelled, "Manny's sick of those jerks on the Reds' team! He wants to be on *our* side!"

Manny didn't like that. He slugged his glove. He stepped up quickly to the rubber, wound up, and *fired*. The pitch was a firecracker, but it almost hit the plate.

Manny shook his head and waved to Winter to hurry and throw the ball back. His coach was telling him to relax, but he aimed the next pitch and it was a floater.

Sterling almost went after it, but it was up even with his eyes.

He took the walk.

Kenny was heading to the plate and everyone was going nuts. The Dodgers were telling him to wait for a good pitch.

Kenny knew that another walk would add to the pressure.

So he let the first pitch go by. But he was mad as soon as it popped into Winter's mitt.

"Steeee-rike one."

The pitch hadn't had much on it, and

Kenny thought he could have mashed it.

Coach Wilkens yelled, "Time this next one, Kenny!"

The Reds were yelling their usual insults about Kenny being a little kid and then screaming, "Batta, batta, batta."

But Kenny watched the ball, timed it, and stroked it perfectly. It shot into left field over the jumping shortstop's head.

Kenny watched the left fielder come toward the ball, field it, and go home with this throw.

Henry had rounded third and was heading for the plate.

The play was going to be close.

Kenny slowed as he made the turn at first. Then he decided he could use the throw home as a chance to go to second.

But he never should have hesitated.

As he sped toward second he heard the crowd scream, heard the ball pop into Winter's mitt, and then . . . *"Ooooouuut!"*

Kenny was running hard. He heard his coach yell, "Slide, Kenny!" and he hit the dirt.

But the throw was right on the money, and Kenny's foot slid directly into the shortstop's glove.

"*Ooooouuut!*" the infield ump yelled.

But someone else was screaming, "*Home! Home! Home!*"

Kenny saw the shortstop spin and throw, and he rolled over to see that Sterling had broken for home on the throw to second.

But he had started late too. The throw home beat him by a mile.

"*Ooooouuut!!!!!*"

Kenny sat up.

But he didn't get up.

A triple play? That couldn't happen.

The Reds were going out of their minds, and the crowd was cheering as though it was the last game of the World Series.

Kenny got up and started walking toward the dugout. As he reached the third-base line, Brian Waters met Kenny and handed him his glove.

Brian was shaking his head. "They lucked out," he said.

But Kenny looked over at his coach, who was still standing near the third-base coach's box.

Coach Wilkens smiled and said, "Well, you gotta hand it to them. They made some great throws."

Kenny didn't like that.

Maybe the coach *didn't* care which team won.

Kenny turned and trotted out to his position. He made up his mind he was going to do something *big* in this game.

He was going to see to it that the Dodgers won—even if the coach thought the Reds were so great.

Kenny had a hard time admitting it himself, but he was starting to think Bunson was right.

Things settled down after all the first-inning fireworks. Bunson was throwing with power *and* control. He got the Reds out one-two-three in the first and again in the second.

In the third, Danny Sandia let a hard-hit grounder get past him for an error. But that guy was the Reds' only base runner.

That was the good news.

The bad news was, the Dodgers couldn't get anything going either.

Manny walked Jenny in the second, and he walked a couple of batters in the third. But each time, the Reds managed to get out of the inning with no runs scored.

The worst part was, Kenny had come up to bat with two runners on in the third, and he had hit another screamer. But he hit it in the air and right at the center fielder.

Then in the fourth, the Dodgers' luck finally changed.

Bunson started off the inning with a hit— a solid shot up the middle.

Manny seemed to get a little rattled again, and he walked Jenny for the second time.

Eddie and Brian both bounced out on easy grounders. But just when it seemed that Manny might slip out of another inning, Billy Bacon hit a high looper in short right field that someone should have caught.

The first and second basemen and the right fielder all ran toward the ball. And then they all stopped at the same time.

It was one of those "You take it—no, *you* take it" plays that always ended up with no one taking it.

The ball dropped on the grass, and two runs scored.

The Dodgers had finally broken on top, and they were psyched.

Lian Jie came up next and hit a hard shot, but the second baseman stabbed it in the air, and so the Reds got out of the inning with only two runs.

But maybe that was all the Dodgers needed. Bunson was mowing down the Reds. The guy meant business today!

★ 4 ★

Battle to the End

Bunson pitched to the Reds' power hitters in the fourth. And he made them look *weak!*

Winter came up to bat with two outs. He waved his bat around like a big shot, and then he pointed a finger at Bunson, as if to say, "Okay, I'll show you."

Bunson used his full motion, but he threw a change-up. Winter swung so hard he spun clear around before the ball even got to him.

Bunson laughed, and so did all the other Dodgers.

Then Bunson fired a fastball at the knees that was by Winter so fast he swung late.

Winter stepped out of the batter's box and slammed his bat on the ground. Then he got back in the box and pushed his helmet down tight.

Bunson threw a fastball that was well outside the strike zone. Poor Winter was too eager by then, and he couldn't stop his swing. He missed the ball by a foot.

Bunson jumped straight up, with his fist in the air. When he came down, he pointed a finger at Winter—the same as Winter had done to him. "Is that the best you can do?" he yelled.

Winter turned and started toward Bunson, but the umpire jumped forward and grabbed him.

"All right," he said. "I'm not putting up with any more of that kind of stuff."

Bunson was still smiling as he walked to the dugout.

But Coach Wilkens stopped him. Kenny heard him say, "You heard the umpire, Rodney. No more of that."

"Winter started it," Bunson said.

"Hey, we've been over this before. I don't *care* who starts it. We're not going to do it."

Kenny saw Bunson look at Sterling and

roll his eyes. Then Bunson walked over and said something to some of the other players.

As Kenny sat down in the dugout he heard him say, "When's the coach going to decide he's on *our* side?"

But everyone forgot all that when Henry hit a shot into the left-center gap. He trotted into second with a stand-up double, and the Dodgers had a chance to add to their lead.

Manny was mad, and he showed it.

He walked Malone.

Kenny was coming up with a chance to do something big for the Dodgers. No triple play this time!

The Reds' coach was walking to the mound. Kenny thought he would only talk to Manny. But Manny slugged his glove angrily and then walked to the dugout.

The big-bellied coach waved to his center fielder to come in to pitch.

This was the kid who had pitched a couple of innings against the Padres and hadn't done very well.

Kenny knew the guy wasn't that good.

But he was also the guy Coach Wilkens had been talking to after the game.

Kenny told himself not to worry about that. The only thing he had to do was get a good pitch and drive it somewhere.

But the new pitcher was bringing his arm over the top and following through. Every warmup pitch was in the strike zone.

Still, he didn't throw all that hard. Kenny would get him.

He stepped up to the plate and took his stance. He held his bat high, and he focused on the pitcher's hand.

The first pitch was on the inside edge of the plate, and Kenny let it go by. The umpire called it a strike.

Kenny wasn't worried.

The next pitch was down in the strike zone but out over the plate. Kenny slammed it hard but on the ground.

Kenny ran all out, but the shortstop fielded the ball and flipped it to the second baseman for the force.

At least Henry was on third with one out. And Bunson was coming up.

But the pitcher kept the ball down again, and Bunson hit another grounder. This time it bounced to Gerstein, the third baseman.

Henry broke for the plate, but it was a mistake. Although the play at home was close, he was out.

Jenny had no more luck. She hit the ball on the ground too, and the shortstop scooped it up and ran to second to make the force on Bunson, unassisted.

So that was that.

The new pitcher had done the job.

And Kenny knew what everyone was thinking. The kid had been terrible in the last game. Coach Wilkens had shown him what he was doing wrong.

Kenny tried not to be mad about it.

And then Bunson ran by him and said, "So now what do you think of Coach Wilkens?"

Kenny didn't answer.

He walked to his position at shortstop and told himself to keep his head in the game.

Bunson was pitching against the guys low in the batting order. He shouldn't have much trouble.

But he was mad, and he started forcing the ball.

He got the new pitcher to pop up to the catcher, but then he struggled to throw strikes and ended up walking a kid who had just come off the bench.

He started out with a couple of balls to another substitute and then got too careful and grooved one that the kid punched into right for a single.

The Reds' bench got really hyped up by that, but Jenny made a great play on a hard-hit grounder. And then Kenny charged a slow ground ball and made a good, quick throw for the out.

So the Dodgers got out of the inning, still ahead 2 to 0.

One more inning.

Kenny knew they were close to cinching at least a tie for the second-half champion-ship. He was excited.

But he was nervous, too.

He didn't like what he had seen happen-ing to Bunson.

The Reds' relief pitcher did a good job again. He kept the ball down, and Eddie and

Jacob both grounded out. Then Harlan, who had been hitting well lately, struck out.

So it all came down to the bottom of the sixth, and the Dodgers needed three outs.

The top of the order was coming up, and the Reds and all their fans were letting Bunson have it. They knew he had trouble when he got mad, and they were really going after him.

Gerstein walked to the plate and yelled, "Hey, Bunson, you're losing your stuff! But don't lose your *temper*."

"Shut up!" Bunson shouted back.

"Oh, no. You *are* losing your temper—and you *know* you can't throw strikes when you do that."

The umpire didn't say anything, and so Coach Wilkens trotted toward home plate. "Let's not have that stuff get started again," he said.

The umpire nodded, and then he said to Gerstein, "Just get up there and bat."

Kenny could see that Bunson's face was turning red—the way it always did when he got upset.

Harlan had come in to catch for Billy, and

Bunson's first pitch was so hard it almost knocked him over. But it was inside.

Bunson never hit the strike zone against Gerstein.

When the umpire called ball four, the Reds went crazy, and Gerstein laughed and waved as he ran to first. "Bunson," he yelled, "thanks for the gift! Got any more for the other guys?"

The Reds' second baseman, a quick little player and a good hitter, was stepping up.

Bunson took a deep breath and then fired a perfect pitch, at the knees.

At least that's how it looked to Kenny.

But the umpire said it was low.

Bunson kicked at the mound and yelled, "What are you talking about, ump?"

That got the Reds' players going again.

On the next pitch he lost the strike zone completely. On a 3 and 0 pitch, he let up and aimed the ball, and the hitter slashed a high, bouncing grounder. Henry charged it and made a great throw, but it was a split second late.

"*Safe!*" the umpire shouted.

Two on.

The tying run was on base and Bunson was losing his cool.

Kenny was scared.

Letter to the Editor

Bunson was furious.

The coach ran out to talk to him. Kenny walked over close enough to hear.

"Rodney," the coach said. "You gotta quit putting so much pressure on yourself. Just tell yourself it's a game and you—"

"I want to *win*—not just *have fun!*" Bunson yelled.

"Sure you do, but you can't let those guys get to you."

Bunson did understand that. He nodded.

"Just relax. You can get these guys."

Bunson listened. He threw a good pitch and the batter bounced a grounder to the right side. Lian snapped up the ball and tossed it to second. Kenny took the throw and fired the ball to first.

They missed the double play by half a step.

But now they had an out.

With runners at first and third, Winter was coming up. He walked toward the plate, but then he yelled, "Time out!"

Suddenly he turned and trotted out toward Bunson. He stopped just a few steps away and said, "Hey, Bunson, don't even *think* about the last game—when *you* blew it, and *I* won the game."

"Shut up, Winter," Bunson said, and he started to turn away.

Kenny was moving toward the mound, afraid of what might happen. The umpire was yelling for Winter to get off the field.

Then Kenny heard Winter say, "You can't help it if you always *choke* just when the game gets tight."

Bunson spun around . . . but then he stopped himself.

Winter turned to walk away, but he looked over his shoulder and said, "Bunson, you're just a *loser*."

Bunson lost it. He charged Winter and tackled him.

The two hit the dirt and rolled over before Kenny could get hold of Bunson.

The umpire helped pull Bunson away. *"All right!"* he yelled. "I told you before. We'll have no more of this."

But the umpire seemed unsure what he should do. He was a young guy. Kenny knew he didn't have all that much experience.

Finally he let go of Bunson and pushed him toward the mound. "One more incident like this, and you're both out of the game."

But Coach Wilkens had hurried over. "What do you mean 'one more incident'? These boys are supposed to be kicked out automatically for fighting."

Kenny almost fell over. What was the coach doing?

"What are you talking about?" the other coach shouted. He was running—or sort of wobbling—onto the field. "My boy wasn't fighting. Bunson went after him."

The umpire hesitated.

Coach Wilkens spoke calmly. "Winter went out on the field and taunted my player. He should be kicked out. My player reacted by tackling him. He should be kicked out too. What are we trying to *teach* these boys?"

"All right," the umpire said firmly. "Both boys are out of the game."

The Reds' coach went crazy, and so did a lot of the fans.

The Dodgers' players were looking around at each other. They couldn't believe what they had seen.

"Kenny, you pitch," Coach Wilkens said. "Get 'em out." He walked off the field.

Bunson lost his temper completely. He and his dad, who had come down to the field, were yelling at the same time.

Coach Wilkens said, "I'll talk to both of you later. But right now I want you to get off the field—we have a game to play."

He walked away from them.

The Reds' coach was still fuming, but he had Manny Tovar come back into the game to bat for Winter.

The Reds' fans were outraged. They screamed for Manny to *murder* the ball.

At the same time the Dodgers and their fans were yelling that Kenny could get the Reds out.

The noise was deafening, and Kenny had never felt so much pressure in his life. The championship was in his hands.

He took a deep breath. He talked to himself. "Don't overthrow. Use your whole body and follow through."

He glanced up at the crowd and saw his dad nodding confidently, telling Kenny with his eyes, "You can do it."

And Kenny made a good pitch. It was hard and low in the strike zone. Manny fouled it off.

Kenny felt better. The next pitch was on the outside corner. Manny let it go and the ump called it a strike.

One more.

Kenny decided to throw his change-up.

But Manny guessed right. He waited on the pitch and *slugged* it.

It was hit long and high in left field.

Still, Kenny thought Eddie would get to it.

But it just kept going. Maybe the wind was blowing out. Maybe the ball had been hit harder than Kenny thought. All he knew for sure was that the ball disappeared over the fence.

That was it.

The game was over. The Reds had won, 3 to 2.

Kenny kept staring out to left, not wanting to face the whole thing—the loss, the disappointment, the other players, his parents. And mostly, those jerks on the Reds' team.

Some of them were already shouting stuff at him. Kenny walked away, and he kept walking—off the field and across the park.

But he didn't make it to the street.

Coach Wilkens ran after him. "Kenny! Kenny!" he yelled.

Kenny didn't turn around, but the coach got in front of him and Kenny stopped.

"Son, you made some great pitches. Manny just—"

"Hit it out of the park."

"I know. But you can't help that."

"I lost the championship," Kenny said. And now he couldn't fight back the tears.

"No, you didn't. You guys played great. It could have gone either way. And we're not out of it yet. We'll end up in a playoff for the season championship. We still may win it."

Kenny didn't dare say what was really on his mind: Why would the coach ask the ump to kick his own player out of the game?

"Don't get down on yourself, Kenny. You've had a great season."

So that was that. The coach didn't seem to be sorry about what he had done. He made no apologies. He didn't even mention Bunson.

Kenny nodded and then he hurried away. He didn't want to walk home with his friends. He didn't want them to see that he'd been crying.

But at school on Monday, Kenny had to face the players. They weren't putting any blame on him, though. They were all mad at Coach Wilkens.

And Kenny couldn't defend him. He knew the coach meant well, but he thought the man owed them more than he was giving.

On Tuesday a letter to the editor appeared in the newspaper. It said what a lot of people around town were saying:

Dear Editor:

On Saturday the Angel Park Dodgers lost a big game that could end up costing them the Little League championship. But a lot of us, including the parents of the players, feel that the kids didn't lose the game. The coach did.

We don't question Coach Wilkens' ability to teach baseball. But we think he ought to get his loyalties straight. He is perfectly willing, at any time, to coach the players from teams in surrounding towns. Those players have their own coaches who would never help the Angel Park kids! Why should he help players our kids play against?

But that sort of thing is mild compared to what he did in the big game Saturday morning. The umpire was happy to warn one of the Dodgers for reacting to a smart-mouthed opponent. But Coach Wilkens convinced the umpire that his *own player* should be kicked out of the game. That player, the star pitcher, left with one out in the sixth inning—and with a shutout going! The Reds went on to win 3 to 2 on a homer that the starting pitcher wouldn't have given up.

Coach Wilkens went too far this time. If he can't fight *for* the Angel Park players, we think he ought to coach somewhere else.

Sincerely,

Concerned Parents of the
Angel Park Dodgers

Kenny knew the letter wasn't really from all the parents. In fact, it was probably only from the Bunsons. But everyone in town read the article, and lots of people thought it made sense.

Kenny wasn't sure.

He did know one thing: one big game was still ahead.

The Giants had won their final game, and that meant the Reds and the Giants were tied for the second-half championship. Those two would play on Wednesday evening, and the winner would play the Dodgers—the first-half champs—on the following Wednesday.

And that game would be for the season championship.

It would all come down to one game.

BOX SCORE, GAME 20

Angel Park Dodgers 2   **Cactus Hills Reds 3**

	ab	r	h	rbi		ab	r	h	rbi
White 3b	2	0	1	0	Gerstein 3b	2	1	0	0
Malone cf	0	0	0	0	Alfonsi 2b	3	1	1	0
Sandoval ss	3	0	1	0	Schulman lf	3	0	0	0
Bunson p	3	1	1	0	Winter c	2	0	0	0
Roper 1b	1	1	0	0	Mendelsohn cf	2	0	0	0
Boschi lf	3	0	0	0	Young ss	1	0	0	0
Waters rf	2	0	0	0	Tovar p	2	1	1	3
Bacon c	1	0	1	2	Lum 1b	2	0	0	0
Sandia 2b	1	0	0	0	Rutter rf	1	0	0	0
Jie 2b	1	0	0	0	Bonthuis 1b	1	0	1	0
Scott rf	1	0	0	0	Higdon rf	0	0	0	0
Sloan c	1	0	0	0	Trulis ss	1	0	0	0
ttl	**19**	**2**	**4**	**2**		**20**	**3**	**3**	**3**

Dodgers	0	0	0	2	0	0—2
Reds	0	0	0	0	0	3—3

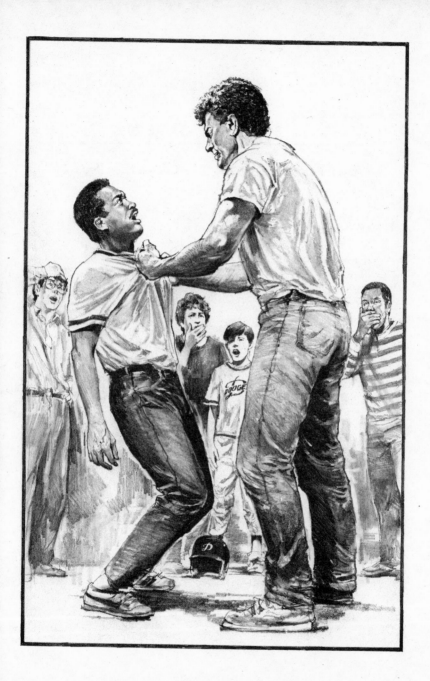

★ 6 ★

This Is It!

Most of the Dodgers' players went to the big play-off game. No one knew for sure whether they wanted the Reds or the Giants to win. It was hard to cheer for either one.

Still, the Giants' "Heat" Halliday was the pitcher the players feared the most. Manny Tovar was good, but he was not as tough as Halliday.

And Heat proved how tough he was that night. Manny had trouble with his control again, and the defense went to pieces. When it was all over, the score was 8 to 3, and Winter was sitting on the bench with his head in his hands.

And there was Cranny Crandall, pointing at the Dodgers, yelling, "You guys are *next!*"

"We'll see about that!" Danny Sandia yelled back at him, but Kenny didn't think he sounded very sure of himself.

What worried Kenny was that the Dodgers were sort of down. Too many kids were still complaining about Coach Wilkens.

School got out for the summer that week and the players started working out at the park every day. By the time Wednesday came around they should have been ready, but they seemed uptight.

Harlan admitted that he was afraid to play. "I'm scared I'm going to lose the championship for us," he told Kenny and Jacob.

"I know. I've been thinking the same thing," Jacob said. "I can't even stand to think about losing to the Giants."

Kenny knew the feeling.

Before the game Coach Wilkens got everyone together at the park, the same as always. But this time he had the parents come over too.

"I want to talk to all of you," he said.

Kenny thought maybe he was finally going to apologize for some of the things he had done.

The players sat on the grass and the parents stood behind them. The coach stood in front, with his hands on his hips.

"I know some of you would rather not see me coach next year, and that's okay. But I hope we'll forget about all that until after this game. Today we need to play together."

"That's right," one of the fathers said.

"But you need to know," the coach continued, "there are things I'm always going to do. I believe Little League is a place to *learn*. I can't resist teaching kids—even if they are on another team."

The coach paused and looked at Mr. Bunson. But Mr. Bunson didn't say anything—though he looked as if he might.

"I'm also never going to allow fighting. If the umpire won't enforce the rule, I will. At least the way I did it the other day, both kids had to leave the game—which was fair."

"I back you on that, one hundred percent," Jacob's mom said, and many of the other parents agreed.

Kenny heard his own dad say, "You did the right thing."

Mr. Bunson didn't look pleased.

"One last thing," the coach said. "Kids want to win—and so do I. The trouble is, they think the whole world is caving in if they make a mistake. But when they're scared, they don't play well. That's why I tell them not to take the game too seriously."

Quite a few of the parents agreed again.

And then a huge voice came from the back. "I don't buy that," the man said.

It wasn't Mr. Bunson. It was . . . the biggest man Kenny had ever seen.

And he was walking around the parents and players and heading for Coach Wilkens.

Kenny's breath caught. The guy looked mad, and he was a monster—the size of a pro-football lineman.

"I'm sick to death of your attitude," the guy said, and he grabbed hold of Coach Wilkens' shirt.

"Wait a minute," the coach said, and he tried to step back. But the guy still had hold of him.

"I'm going to punch your lights out," the big guy said, and he pulled back his huge fist and let it fly.

The coach jerked his head to the side and the fist went right on by.

A couple of the fathers were trying to get to the guy to grab him. The kids were all stunned.

But Coach Wilkens suddenly jumped back and then charged forward and rammed his head right into the guy's gut.

Wham.

The man let out a huge grunt and went sprawling across the grass. And he stayed down. He didn't even move.

Maybe five seconds went by, and the whole world seemed silent. Kenny couldn't believe what the coach had just done.

And then he saw the smile.

The coach turned toward the kids and said, "I dodged him, right? That makes me a dodger. And you can see that this guy is a giant. Now you know what *Dodgers* do to *Giants*."

At the same moment the giant suddenly

"awoke" and got to his feet. His laugh was big enough to fill all of Angel Park.

Everyone was still staring at the coach. What the heck was going on?

That's when Coach Wilkens said, "I want you to meet my friend Gus. I talked him into helping me out here a little today. Now what about it? Can Dodgers knock down Giants or not?"

The Dodgers didn't answer. They were still getting used to the idea that Coach Wilkens had been tricking them all along.

But then Billy started to laugh, and suddenly everyone was cracking up.

The parents laughed almost as hard as the kids. Even Mr. Bunson.

The coach waited for at least a minute, and then he said, "Okay. Let's have some fun. And let's beat those Giants. But don't butt 'em with your heads. Beat 'em with base hits."

The players were suddenly on their feet, still laughing but cheering too, and then they headed out onto the field.

"Remember," Coach Wilkens yelled after

them, "no smart stuff! No fighting. No arguing. Let's show some class today. We're champs."

Across the field the Giants' players were wondering what in the world was going on.

Kenny felt really good for the first time in a long while. He felt as if the team . . . was a team again.

The crowd was huge. People were sitting everywhere. And Kenny was excited.

But he kept telling himself, "Don't get uptight. Relax. Have fun." And he kept thinking about the coach letting that "Giant" have it in the gut. He couldn't help laughing.

He took some ground balls and made some good throws to Jenny. And he glanced over and saw that Bunson was really firing, looking good.

Somehow, he felt that this was their night.

And then Cranny tried to start some trouble.

"Hey, Bunson," he yelled, "is that your best fastball? Heat throws *twice* that hard."

Bunson knew what to do—ignore that

stuff. But Cranny had a cocky way about him that could drive a guy crazy.

And Crandall kept it up. "Don't get mad, whatever you do, Bunson. You know you don't pitch good when you get mad."

Bunson didn't say a word, but he wasn't smiling anymore either.

Coach Wilkens saw what was happening. He ran to the mound.

Kenny walked over too.

"Rodney," Coach Wilkens said, "you're a great pitcher. The best Little League pitcher I've ever coached."

"Really?" Bunson said.

"Really." The coach nodded. "Halliday is tough. But he relies mostly on his speed. You have better control—until you get mad, or until you try to force the ball."

Bunson nodded. Kenny could see that he was pleased.

"Just relax and throw and you'll get these guys out. Can you trust in that?"

Bunson was nodding. "Yeah."

Kenny liked what he saw. Bunson looked calm now.

"All right. Let's win the championship, and let's have fun doing it. You're a good kid, Rodney. Remember, we're going to show some class today."

Bunson and the coach shook hands.

And then the coach ran off the field.

This was it. Game time.

"Hey, Bunson!" Kenny yelled, and Bunson looked over. "Remember what Dodgers do to Giants?"

Bunson laughed. And then he looked in to get his sign. He was ready to start the big game—for the *championship*.

★ 7 ★

Burner and Heat

Bunson looked great in the first inning. The Giants screamed at him nonstop. But he moved the ball around, struck out two batters, and got tough-hitting Dave Weight on a grounder.

But Heat was just as tough.

He mowed down White and Malone. And then Kenny came up. Kenny took a good swing. But he was late getting around on Halliday's fastball. He popped the ball up in foul territory. The first baseman made the catch.

The second and third innings went the same way. Neither team got a runner on base. Bunson threw three screaming fastballs right past Cranny Crandall.

But Cranny didn't know enough to shut his mouth. When his team came up in the top of the fourth, he was all over Bunson again. So were all the Giants.

Tension was mounting.

Bunson didn't lose his cool. He made a good pitch, but the Giants' leadoff batter got his bat on it. He didn't hit it hard, but it blooped into right field for a single.

Bunson bore down then, and he struck out the second batter. But Weight was up again.

Bunson was a little too careful on his first two pitches and got behind, 2 and 0.

Kenny saw Billy, who was catching, set up his target on the outside, but Bunson let his pitch come in over the middle of the plate.

Weight laced the ball hard into center field.

Malone charged. He fielded the ball, grabbed for it . . . but dropped it. The speedy base runner rounded third and scored.

Kenny screamed, "*Second! Second!*" and ran to the bag.

Weight had expected Malone to go home with the ball. He was steaming toward second.

The ball got to Kenny ahead of the runner, but Weight slid hard, slamming into Kenny's leg.

Kenny went down, but he held on to the ball.

"Ooooouuut!" the umpire called.

But a run had scored. The Giants had gone ahead.

And there was one other problem.

Kenny got up, but his right ankle had twisted in the collision. He took a step on it and then dropped to the ground.

Coach Wilkens ran out quickly.

The crowd was suddenly quiet.

Then, in the quiet, Cranny's voice rang out. "What's the matter, you little boob? He didn't hit you that hard."

Kenny got up again, took another step. The pain was letting up some. "It's okay," he said.

"Are you sure?" asked the coach.

"Yeah. I twisted it a little, but it's okay."

Bunson had come over. He pounded his fist in his glove. "That jerk didn't have to slide so hard," he said.

"No," Kenny said. "I didn't straddle the bag the way I'm supposed to. I let my leg get in his way."

"Come on, *wimp!*" Cranny yelled. "You gonna *play* or *cry?*"

Bunson spun around, but the coach grabbed his shoulder. "Don't let him get to you. We're only down by one."

Bunson nodded and went back to the mound. Kenny used all his control to walk back to his position without limping.

Bunson kept his cool. But his pitches were burning.

The next batter slapped a hard grounder up the middle. That was no problem. Speedy Lian Jie gobbled up the ball like a pro and tossed the ball over to Jenny for the out.

Now the Dodgers needed to start getting to Halliday.

Things looked better when Henry fouled off a couple of pitches, took some, and then walked on a 3 and 2 pitch.

Finally, a base runner.

And then Malone proved that Heat could be hit.

He lined the first pitch past Weight at third.

Henry had to stop at second, but Kenny was coming up with no outs and two runners on base.

He tried not to show his pain, but when he took his batting position, he had to shift his weight more to his front foot, and he felt awkward.

He let a pitch go by, but the ump called it a strike. The next pitch was in on his hands, but he swung. He felt wrong, off-balance, and the ball bounced straight back to Halliday.

Kenny ran hard.

Heat played it smart and went to third for the force out. Kenny ended up on first base on the fielder's choice.

But as he crossed the bag and slowed up, he felt the pain grab again—as bad as it had at the very first.

And now he knew he had to make a decision.

He wanted to play more than anything in the world.

But it wasn't right.

"Time out!" he yelled. He walked to the coach, but he could no longer stop himself from limping.

"Coach, maybe you ought to put someone in for me."

"Okay. I could tell you were hurting when you went down the first-base line."

The coach yelled for Danny to run for Kenny. But as Kenny turned to leave, Coach Wilkens said, "Kenny, you did the right thing. You're thinking about the team, not just yourself."

Kenny felt good about that, but he felt terrible about not playing. He hoped now that Bunson could come through.

And Bunson did. He hit a rocket—right past the first baseman.

Sterling scored from second and Danny scored all the way from first. The Dodgers had the lead!

Kenny knew for sure now that he had made a good decision. He never would have made it all the way to home with that bad ankle.

And now his team was up by a run. He just hoped they could keep the rally going.

The Dodgers were all shouting for Jenny to knock the ball out of the park. She didn't do that, but she hit a hard grounder to deep short. The shortstop had no chance to throw her out.

Bunson moved to third.

Runners were now at the corners with only one out.

Jacob Scott was coming up. He had just gone into the game for Brian Waters.

Cranny got all over Jacob. "Look out, little boy," he kept saying. "Heat's *mad* now."

But Jacob played it smart. He let Heat throw a couple of pitches hard and inside and get behind in the count. When the count worked to 3 and 1, Heat took something off his fastball. Jacob was ready. He took an easy swing and poked the ball into right field.

Bunson scored.

In the dugout the Dodgers went nuts.

Harlan was bouncing around yelling, "Way

to go, Jacob! Show 'em what the rookies can do."

And Kenny was hopping on one foot, slapping Harlan on the back and yelling to Jacob.

Jacob was grinning from his toes up, his split teeth showing all the way from first base.

Bunson walked into the dugout. He high-fived everyone as he made his way through.

But then the coach yelled, "Harlan, bat for Billy!"

Bunson spun around. "No, don't . . ."

He didn't finish his sentence. Kenny could see that he was sorry he had reacted.

But he also knew Harlan had heard. "*Do it*, Harlan!" Kenny yelled. "We *all* make it happen today."

Harlan walked to the box. He looked as if he meant business.

He swung at the first pitch and hit a hotshot grounder. For a moment it looked as though the shortstop might get it, but the ball bounced off his glove.

The second baseman ran it down, and no

runs scored, but the bases were now loaded.

Lian was up.

"Come on! Come through, Line Drive!" Bunson yelled.

Lian was smiling, the way he always did. He even smiled at Cranny, who was telling him that he was a midget who couldn't swing a bat.

But he did swing his bat, and he hit a line drive for a single.

Two runs scored, and the Dodgers were up 5 to 1.

No one could stop them now!

★ 8 ★

It Ain't Over till It's Over

But someone forgot to tell the Giants that the game was all locked up.

Kenny knew Halliday had made up his mind not to let the game get out of hand. He started throwing real flames! He got Eddie Boschi on a strikeout and Henry on a fly ball.

Then he batted first in the fifth inning. He stepped up to the plate and smacked Bunson's first pitch into the left field corner. He ran hard and slid into second for a double.

Kenny felt his stomach tighten. Sitting on the bench was ten times worse than playing.

And then he saw his dad coming his way. "I just ran and got some tape," he said. "I want to tape that ankle."

"Why?"

"The coach might need you again."

While his dad was taping the ankle, Kenny heard the ping of a metal bat. He looked up to see Halliday rounding third and heading home.

"Oh, *no!*" Kenny said.

His dad grinned at him. "It's fun. Remember."

"We can't lose *now*. We've got it if we can just hold on."

"Well, getting all nervous and worried won't help a bit."

Just then Kenny heard *"Steeee-rike three!"* The Dodgers' fans roared. Bunson was staying tough.

And by the time Dad had finished taping, Bunson had struck out another guy.

Kenny felt a lot better. He could put weight on his ankle without a lot of pain, and Bunson was getting them out.

But Cranny was coming up to bat.

And he was yelling something at Bunson.

Bunson threw a real smoker. But it was high and Harlan had to go way up for it.

Cranny's mouth was still going, and Kenny knew that Bunson wanted more than anything to strike him out.

But that was the problem. He was pressing too hard again. He wasn't all that wild, but Cranny waited him out, and he finally got a walk on a close call.

Cranny's mouth never stopped. When he reached first base, he yelled, "You're *shot*, Bunson. You're falling apart."

Coach Wilkens shouted at the same time, "Rodney, relax!" He gave Bunson a big smile.

Bunson nodded, but he didn't smile.

The leadoff batter was stepping in.

Bunson took a long breath. He said something to himself, and then he stepped up to the rubber and fired a pitch on the outside edge and down in the strike zone.

The batter took a good swing but hit the ball off the end of the bat. It skittered toward the right side.

Lian charged, scooped it, spun, and threw.

The Dodgers were out of the inning and still ahead 5 to 2.

"Let's get some more runs!" all the Dodgers were yelling.

Malone, Sandia, and Bunson were coming up. It seemed a great time to break the game wide open.

But Heat had his rhythm back. He got the Dodger hitters out in order.

So it all came down to the final inning.

Three more outs.

As the Dodgers ran back to the field the coach was clapping and shouting, "Okay, kids, this is what it's all about. Enjoy it."

The Giants' coach was screaming his head off. "Do you kids *want* it or don't you? You don't act like you do. I want to see some *hitters* up there."

"Three outs," Kenny whispered to himself. But he wasn't sure this was fun. He couldn't stand still, he was so nervous.

Bunson looked sweet against the first batter. The kid just stood there, taking strikes, praying for a walk. The walk didn't come—and now there were only two outs to go.

But it was Dave Weight who was coming

up. The kid was a natural, and Bunson didn't seem to scare him.

Bunson came with a fastball that was a little high, and then he tried his curve. Weight stayed with it and knocked it into right field for a single.

The noise level shot way up. Insults rained down on Bunson.

Kenny didn't like what he saw. Bunson was suddenly struggling again. That hit had upset him, or maybe it was something someone had yelled. Red blotches started to appear on his neck and cheeks.

Bunson took some long, deep breaths. He nodded when the coach told him to take it easy.

His first pitch to Dodero was close but a little high. The Reds' players went crazy. Each pitch after that was higher than the last one.

And when Dodero trotted down to first base with a walk, the tying run was coming to the plate.

It was Halliday!

Cranny was going wild in the dugout. "You're finished, Bunson. You're finished. You have no control. It's gone. It's *gone*. It's *gone*. You're *finished*."

And the other players picked up the chant. "Bunson, you're *finished*. Bunson, you're *finished*."

Bunson slammed the ball into his glove, stepped on the rubber, and got his sign. But he waited a long time—and then he stepped back.

The chant picked up, louder and louder. "Bunson, you're *finished!* Bunson, you're *finished!*"

Suddenly Bunson called time out. He trotted over toward the coach. At the same time he yelled, "Kenny, come here."

Kenny had no idea what was going on, but he ran out to where Bunson and the coach were standing, near the third-base line.

"Coach," Bunson said. "I've been throwing too hard. My arm is tired. And I'm letting those guys get to me. I was thinking Kenny could pitch—now that he's got his ankle taped."

The coach gave it some thought before he said, "What about it, Kenny?"

"I think I could do it. My ankle isn't too bad. But Bunson's a better pitcher. I think he can get 'em."

Kenny meant it, too. He knew he couldn't throw as hard as Bunson.

The coach thought for a time, and he kept watching Bunson. "I appreciate your telling the truth about your arm, Rodney. I'd rather have you stay in, but if your arm is getting tired, let's have Kenny finish them off."

He took the ball from Bunson and handed it to Kenny.

Kenny felt his stomach do a flip, but he nodded and started toward the mound. He heard the coach say behind him, "I'm proud of you guys—no matter what happens."

Kenny took his warmup pitches.

And now the chant had changed. "No *rookie* is gonna beat us. Go back to kindergarten, rookie!"

Kenny tried not to listen, but his hands were sweating and his stomach was still doing flips and flops.

He finally stared in at Harlan's glove and tried to forget it was Halliday up to bat. But he could hear those guys yelling, and something inside him was saying, "I can't be the loser again—not in the championship game."

He stepped off the rubber. He tried to clear his mind. But the chanting never stopped.

When he finally pitched the ball, it got away from him. It bounced on the grass and then off Harlan's shin guard.

The runners moved up.

"Okay, you got that out of your system. It doesn't matter!" the coach yelled. "Forget those guys. They can score. Just get Halliday."

But the chant was still going, all the noise, and Kenny knew the whole season—everything they had worked for—was on his shoulders.

He wound up and threw hard, but the ball was outside. Harlan had to dive to stop it.

You can't do this, Kenny told himself. You gotta settle down.

He walked behind the mound and looked away. He tried to get his breathing under control.

When he turned around he saw Heat, glaring at him, looking as though he wanted to *kill* him.

He wished he had never gotten into this mess. He almost wished he had never started playing baseball.

★9★

Are We Having Fun Yet?

Then Kenny noticed his dad. He had come down to the fence. He was smiling—a big overdone sort of grin—and he was pointing to his mouth. "Smile!" he yelled.

Oh, sure, Kenny told himself. In fact, Kenny felt himself getting angry. Didn't Dad understand what he was going through?

"That's right. Smile!" Coach Wilkens yelled. "Have some fun. You know what you can do."

The Giants were screaming themselves hoarse.

"Smile, Kenny!" they were all yelling.

But over the noise a big voice bellowed, "Hey, Kenny!" Kenny glanced over at the dugout. "Remember what Dodgers do to Giants!" Bunson yelled.

Bunson had little Lian Jie by the shirt, and he took a big swing. Lian dodged, jumped back, and then ran at Bunson. Bunson took a wild, fake fall and ended up flat on his back.

Kenny couldn't help smiling a little.

But the umpire was yelling at him to get going, and Kenny still knew what he had to face.

And then he heard that deep voice of Jacob's, booming in from right field. "Look at Cranny. That'll make you *laugh*."

Kenny did look at Cranny. The guy was screaming like a maniac. His face was all red, and his eyes were bulging. Kenny wondered whether the kid was losing his mind!

And the whole thing suddenly did seem funny. The guy was acting as if the world was about to end. How could he be *that* upset—over a baseball game?

Kenny hadn't realized what a big smile had spread across his face until the Giants reacted.

"What are you grinning about, little kid?" Halliday yelled.

And at about the same time the ump yelled, "Come on, young man, pitch the ball!"

Kenny nodded and stepped to the rubber. He smiled at Heat, who was still trying to stare him down.

Then he threw a nice pitch, not all that hard, but in a good spot, on the outside corner.

Halliday swung for the fence. But he didn't get the fat of the bat on the ball. He hit a high fly into right field.

Jacob took a step back. But then he realized that the ball wasn't going to carry. He took off hard toward the infield.

At the same time Danny was running hard toward right, with his back to the infield. Both were closing in on the ball, and for a moment it seemed they might crash into each other. But Jacob yelled, "I got it!" and stretched out his arm.

Danny ducked just as the ball struck Jacob's glove. Jacob had the ball, but he crashed into Danny and went head over heels.

There was one everlasting second before he got back to his feet, holding his glove high in the air.

The ball was still in it.

The whole crowd seemed to take a deep breath, and then the umpire shouted, *"Oooooouuuuuuuuut!"*

The umpire's voice was sweet music.

Jacob ran toward the infield, making sure the runner on third didn't try to score.

Two outs. Halliday gone. The championship was one out away.

"Hey, Jacob!" Kenny yelled. "Great catch—for a rookie!"

Jacob grinned and waved two fingers. "Two down!" he yelled. "One to go."

Kenny was really smiling now. Maybe the game *was* fun.

But the Giants could hardly face the idea that they could lose. They kept screaming at the Glenn kid who played first base that he *had* to come through.

Kenny saw exactly what was happening. The Giants were putting all the pressure on themselves. The poor batter didn't have a chance.

Kenny looked over at the coach, smiled, and nodded.

He was in control. The first pitch was on the inside corner, and Glenn jumped back, faking that it was close to him. He wanted a walk, but the umpire called a strike. He didn't want to make the last out and have his whole team on his back.

The next pitch was on the outside edge and Glenn let it go by again.

Strike two.

"You *idiot!*" Cranny yelled. "Don't just stand there and let him throw strikes past you!"

And Kenny knew he had him. This was it.

He broke off his curve, and Glenn swung so hard he almost knocked himself down. But he ticked the ball—and it rolled in front of the plate.

Glenn took off for first.

Harlan jumped from behind the plate, stumbled a little, but grabbed the ball. He was off-balance as he came up, but he cocked his arm to throw.

Then he realized what he was doing. He

had time. He pulled the ball back, stepped up and got his balance, and then *fired* the ball to first.

Jenny caught it, and it was all over!

The *championship.*

Kenny leaped high in the air.

The *championship.*

"We did it! We did it!" he was yelling.

The *championship.*

People were suddenly jumping all over Kenny. He was at the bottom of a heap of kids, arms and legs crisscrossing him, and screams and yells filling his ears.

The *championship.*

"Way to go, Kenny! Way to go!" kids were yelling.

The *championship.*

Kenny just lay there and let himself get smashed. And all he could think was: The *championship.*

But once the players rolled off him, he had some things he had to do.

First, no matter what had happened, he knew he had to slap hands with the Giants. He told Heat that he was a *great* pitcher. And he meant it.

Heat, of course, told him to shut his mouth.

Kenny smiled about that.

Cranny was sitting in the dugout crying, so Kenny left him alone. But he told Dave Weight and some of the other Giants what a good team they had.

Then he found his dad and mom. He jumped into his dad's arms, and his dad swung him around a couple of times. Then his mom grabbed him up and swung him herself.

"You were great," she told him.

But Kenny said, "You were right, Dad. It *was* fun."

Then Kenny had to find Bunson and thank him. But he couldn't think what to say, so he just high-fived him and said, "I wish you had another year with us."

Kenny also found the coach, and he knew exactly what he wanted to say this time. "Coach Wilkens, we won the game before the last out, didn't we?"

"Yes. Yes," the coach said, nodding over and over. "Now you understand what I've been trying to tell you. The game is usually won or lost right up here." He tapped his head with his finger.

"You've been right the whole time," Kenny said.

The coach grinned and slapped hands with Kenny.

And then, most important, Kenny found Jacob and Harlan. The three looked at each other and laughed.

Kenny put his hand out, and they all knew what that meant. They leaped out of their skins, it seemed, and slammed hands, three ways, up in the air.

And for a moment it seemed to Kenny as though they would never come down.

But they all landed—safely—and then Jacob said, "Just think how fun *next year* is going to be. We won't be rookies anymore. We'll be *defending champs!*"

Suddenly the boys were back in the air, leaping high.

We *got* it, Kenny kept telling himself. We're *stars*.

BOX SCORE, CHAMPIONSHIP GAME

Blue Springs Giants 2

	ab	r	h	rbi
Nugent lf	3	1	1	0
Sanchez ss	2	0	0	0
Weight 3b	3	0	2	1
Dodero cf	2	0	0	0
Halliday p	3	1	1	0
Glenn 1b	3	0	1	1
Zonn rf	1	0	0	0
Cooper 2b	1	0	0	0
Crandall c	1	0	0	0
Villareal rf	1	0	0	0
Hausberg 2b	1	0	0	0
Spinner ss	1	0	0	0
ttl	**22**	**2**	**5**	**2**

Angel Park Dodgers 5

	ab	r	h	rbi
White 3b	2	0	0	0
Malone cf	3	1	1	0
Sandoval ss	2	0	0	0
Bunson p	3	1	1	2
Roper 1b	2	1	1	0
Waters rf	1	0	0	0
Bacon c	1	0	0	0
Jie 2b	2	0	1	2
Boschi lf	2	0	0	0
Sandia ss	1	1	0	0
Scott rf	1	1	1	1
Sloan c	1	0	1	0
	21	**5**	**6**	**5**

Giants	0	0	0	1	1	0—2	
Dodgers	0	0	0	5	0	x—5	

League standings after ten games
(second half of season)

Giants	7–3
Reds	7–3
Dodgers	6–4
A's	4–6
Mariners	4–6
Padres	2–8

Ninth game scores

Dodgers	13	Mariners	5
A's	7	Giants	6
Reds	6	Padres	3

Tenth game scores

Reds	3	Dodgers	2
Giants	9	Padres	6
A's	6	Mariners	1

Play-off, second-half championship

Giants	8	Reds	3

League championship

Dodgers	5	Giants	2

ENTER THE ANGEL PARK ALL-STARS SWEEPSTAKES!

- The Grand Prize: a trip for four to the 1991 All-Star Game in Toronto
- 25 First Prizes: Louisville Slugger Little League bat personalized with the winner's name and the Angel Park All-Stars logo

See official entry rules below.

OFFICIAL RULES—NO PURCHASE NECESSARY

1. On an official entry form print your name, address, zip code, age, and the answer to the following question: What are the names of the three main characters in the Angel Park All-Stars books? The information needed to answer this question can be found in any of the Angel Park All-Stars books, or you may obtain an entry form, a set of rules, and the answer to the question by writing to: Angel Park Request, P.O. Box 3352, Syosset, NY 11775-3352. Each request must be mailed separately and must be received by November 1, 1990.

2. Enter as often as you wish, but each entry must be mailed separately to: ANGEL PARK ALL-STARS SWEEPSTAKES, P.O. Box 3335, Syosset, NY 11775-3335. No mechanically reproduced entries will be accepted. All entries must be received by December 1, 1990.

3. **Winners will be selected, from among correct entries received, in a random drawing conducted by National Judging Institute, Inc., an independent judging organization whose decisions are final on all matters relating to this sweepstakes. All prizes will be awarded and winners notified by mail. Prizes are nontransferable, and no substitutions or cash equivalents are allowed. Taxes, if any, are the responsibility of the individual winners. Winners may be asked to verify address or execute an affidavit of eligibility and release. No responsibility is assumed for lost, misdirected, or late entries or mail. Grand Prize consists of a three-day/two-night trip for a family of four to the 1991 All-Star Game in Toronto, Canada, including round-trip air transportation, hotel accommodations, game tickets, hotel-to-airport and hotel-to-game transfers, and breakfasts and dinners. In the event the trip is won by a minor, it will be awarded in the name of a parent or legal guardian. Trip must be taken on date specified or the prize will be forfeited and an alternate winner selected. RANDOM HOUSE, INC., and its affiliates reserve the right to use the prize winners' names and likenesses in any promotional activities relating to this sweepstakes without further compensation to the winners.**

4. Sweepstakes open to residents of the U.S. and Canada, except for the Province of Quebec. Employees and their families of RANDOM HOUSE, INC., and its affiliates, subsidiaries, advertising agencies, and retailers, and Don Jagoda Associates, Inc., may not enter. This offer is void wherever prohibited, and subject to all federal, state, and local laws.

5. **For a list of winners, send a stamped, self-addressed envelope to: ANGEL PARK WINNERS, P.O. Box 3347, Syosset, NY 11775-3347.**

....

Angel Park All-Stars Sweepstakes Official Entry Form

Name:_____ Age:_____
      (Please Print)

Address_____

City/State/Zip:_____

What are the names of the three main characters in the Angel Park All-Stars books?

_____